DIARY OF A MINECRAFT ZOMBIE

BOOK 5

SCHOOL DAZE

Koala Books
An imprint of Scholastic Australia Pty Limited
PO Box 579 Gosford NSW 2250
ABN 11 000 614 577
www.scholastic.com.au

Part of the Scholastic Group
Sydney • Auckland • New York • Toronto • London • Mexico City
• New Delhi • Hong Kong • Buenos Aires • Puerto Rico

First published by Zack Zombie Publishing in 2015.
Published by Scholastic Australia in 2017.
Text copyright © Zack Zombie Publishing 2017.

A catalogue record for this
book is available from the
National Library of Australia

NATIONAL
LIBRARY
OF AUSTRALIA

ISBN 978-1-74381-831-2

Typeset in Agent 'C' and Potato Cut TT

Printed in China by Hang Tai Printing Company Limited.

Scholastic Australia's policy, in association with Hang Tai Printing Company, is to
use papers that are renewable and made efficiently from wood grown in responsibly
managed forests, so as to minimise its environmental footprint.

23 24 25 / 2

BOOK 5

SCHOOL DAZE

BY
Zack Zombie

Koala Books

☀ SUNDAY ☀

I can't believe it!

It's almost here.

Just a few more weeks until **SCARE-CATION** begins, which means no more Scare School! That means no more teachers, no more books and no more Villagers giving me dirty looks...

And no more going out and scaring Villagers for an entire summer.

Now, don't get me wrong. I like scaring the occasional Villager. Especially when they drop cool stuff like cake, or a Bow and Arrow or something like that. But nothing beats being able to do whatever you want during scare-cation.

I was trying to think about what I would be going to do for scare-cation. I was thinking of just playing video games and eating cake **ALL DAY** and doing that every day for the next three months.

But I was sure my mum and dad

were not going to let me have
that much fun. They seemed to
think that ruining my scare-cation
was part of their Zombie parent
job description or something.

Or I was thinking of just spending
my whole summer hanging out with
Skelee, Slimey and Creepy. We
would get into all kinds of trouble.

But there wasn't a lot of trouble we
could get into in a small village like
the one we lived in. Maybe we could
play with **A FEW SPIDERS** or
knock on the Witch's door and run

away. But after the first day, we would've already done everything! We will have to find out what to do with the rest of the summer.

My mum and dad said they were thinking of sending me to camp over the summer. But there's no way I'm going to spend part of my summer doing crafts and eating **GROSS CAMP FOOD.**

Plus, I would probably miss all my friends, and Sally and Steve.

I just have to make sure that I get a good report from Scare

School so my parents don't punish me by sending me to camp.

Anyway, all I know is that I **CAN'T WAIT** for school to finish. All I have to do is get through the next few weeks and I'm free!

M✱NDAY

A lot of the kids at school today were talking about what they were going to do this summer.

Skelee said that his parents were going to take him to Yellowbone National Park. I think he said that was where his parents were from.

Slimey said he was going to the Superflat Biome. He said they have **BIG FIELDS** where he can have fun and jump around.

Creepy said his parents were sending him away to camp. I felt really bad for Creepy. But he said he's been going to camp for the past three years. He said he liked camp because they make **COOL CRAFTS,** play lots of sports and eat really good food.

Sometimes I think Creepy is living in another world...

The guys asked me what I was doing for summer. I just told them I was going to play video games and eat cake all summer.

'I wish I could do that,' Skelee said. 'But my parents always ruin it. I think they feel like if they let me have fun, then they're not being good Skeleton parents or something.'

I'm really going to **MISS MY FRIENDS** over the summer. But I think Steve is going to be around so I'll hang out with him.

I went to go visit Steve to see what he was up to. I found him night fishing by the lake.

'Hey, Steve!' I said.

'AAAAAHHH!!!' Steve screamed. 'Zombie, why do you always sneak up on me like that?!'

'I've been practising for my Scare Class exam that's coming up in a few weeks,' I said.

'Oh, that makes sense. By the way,' Steve said, 'I was just thinking of something I wanted to ask you. Why did your parents name you Zombie? Why didn't they call you JOE OR EDGAR or something like that?'

'Zombie is not my real name.

That's just a nickname people call me,' I said. 'My real name is Zack. Zack Zombie.'

'ZACK ZOMBIE, really?'

'Yeah, most Zombies have the last name Zombie,' I said.

Like my uncle Harry Zombie or my neighbour Seymour Zombie.

There are a few kids at school with the name Zombie too. There's:

- [x] **Ima Zombie**
- [x] **Ada Zombie**
- [x] **Major Zombie**

- [x] Nada Zombie
- [x] Norma Lee Zombie
- [x] Sacha Zombie
- [x] Ivana Zombie
- [x] So Yung Zombie
- [x] Zeena Zombie
- [x] Yuri Zombie

There's even a kid named Zombie Zombie.

'Oh, so Zombie is kind of like **SMITH OR JONES** for Humans,' Steve said.

'I guess,' I said. 'Is your last name Smith?'

'No... actually, I don't know my last name.'

'**WHOA,**' I said. 'But I bet if you did, it would be something cool like "Steve Human" or something like that.'

Steve just looked at me... confused.

TUESDAY

Tomorrow is Picture Day. That's when we take pictures for our **SCHOOL YEARBOOK.**

I don't like taking pictures. No matter how I smile, I always end up looking really silly.

My awkward smile ⤳

Big-mouth Jeff always looks really good in his pictures. And this year he got lucky. He got a case of the **CHICKEN POX** right before Picture Day. Now, he's going to look really awesome.

A lot of the other kids got chicken pox too. But for some reason I just couldn't catch it.

All the other kids caught all the cool diseases like:

- **Measles**
- **Mumps**
- **Chicken pox**
- **Small pox**

Some of the kids at school even caught some cool flesh-eating diseases too. But for some reason, I couldn't get any.

It's like the **ONLY DISEASE** I ever catch is a case of bad luck.

WEDNESDAY

My mum got me a new outfit for Picture Day today.

It's a good thing that Picture Day is only once a year. Mum just doesn't know what it means to look cool! I thought I looked really lame. It would be my worst DAYMARE to look like this more than once a year!

When I got to school all the kids were dressed in their best clothes. I had never seen mobs look so good.

And then big-mouth Jeff and his crew arrived, all covered in chicken pox... and they looked awesome.

I wanted to look awesome too! So I decided to **FAKE THE MEASLES.**

Hey, I couldn't get the chicken pox but I thought that's the least I could do.

So, I took a red marker from my teacher's desk and I ran to the bathroom. But the bathroom was full of mob kids getting ready for their photos. So, I ran to the janitor's closet instead.

There was **NO MIRROR** in
there so I just started dotting my
face with the marker.

Man, this is gonna look so good,
I thought.

Once I was finished, I walked out
of the janitor's closet. I was so
proud of my measles that I decided
to strut down the hall so that
everyone could see me.

All of a sudden, all the kids
started staring at me and giggling.

Some kids even started laughing out loud!

I caught my reflection in the window and I was so shocked. I had accidentally dotted my face with a black marker, instead of a red one!

I knew it was weird that the marker cap was red and the rest of it was black.

My face looked like a green and black **CHECKERBOARD.**

I ran as fast as I could to the bathroom to wash it off, but the bathroom was still full. So I ran back to the janitor's closet again.

Just my luck!

When I tried to use the sink, it was broken. Then I saw a big **BOTTLE** of something that had liquid in it.

It had an old label that was really hard to read. I think it read, 'BLE-CH'.

It sounded like something you'd use if you felt like your face looked 'blech'.

So I soaked a rag into the bottle
and rubbed my face over and over
again. I had to rub really hard to
get the marker off because it was
permanent. It was weird because
by the time I finished the rag
was full of all kinds of colours
including black, green and red.

But I was just glad I got it off.

So, I walked outside and did my
strut down the hallway. This time,
no-one was laughing but they
sure were staring at me with the
BIGGEST EYE SOCKETS

I had ever seen.

Man, I must look really good,
I thought.

I walked into the room where
they were taking pictures and the
photographer's eye sockets grew
really big too.

'Are you sure you want your
picture taken?' he asked.

I guess he thought I missed a
button on my shirt or something.

'**GO FOR IT!**' I said proudly.

'Okay,' he said while giving me a weird look. Then he took my picture.

Man, I can't wait until the yearbook comes out. This picture is going to look so **AWESOME!**

☀ THURSDAY ☀

Stayed home from school to grow my face back today.

Ouch...

My mum said it was probably the flash from the camera that made my face **MELT OFF** like that.

'I guess my baby is just a sensitive soul,' she said.

Oh brother...

FRIDAY

Today at school, we had to write an essay about what we were planning to do for the summer. I was going to write about how I was going to stay home all summer to play video games and eat cake. But I didn't want my teacher to tell my mum and dad at the **PARENT-TEACHER CONFERENCE** tonight.

I really don't like parent-teacher conferences.

I think teachers and parents probably get together to plot ways to ruin all the kids' summers.

I could imagine the Principal getting up on the stage and saying, 'Okay everyone. How can we make sure we **RUIN THE KIDS' SUMMER** this year?'

'Make sure they have lots of chores to do!' somebody would say.

'Make sure you invite all of your weird relatives to stay with you for the summer... and make sure you give them the kid's room to sleep in,' another person would say.

And of course somebody is going to say, '**SEND THEM AWAY** to camp for the whole summer, where they can do crafts and eat nasty camp food.'

That would probably be the one idea that everybody was going to agree with.

Then I realised that if I just wrote my essay about 'how much I love camp' instead of my plan to play video games and have a cake marathon, then my teacher wouldn't have anything to say and wouldn't reveal my scare-cation plans to my parents at the parent-teacher conference tonight.

It was genius!

So I wrote my whole essay on how cool it would be to go to camp for the summer. I wrote about how much I loved to do crafts, especially lanyards and macaroni pictures. I wrote about how great the camp food would be. I even wrote about how camp would be a great way for me to **MAKE NEW FRIENDS** for the summer.

I'm sure with an essay like that, my teacher will be totally fooled and not tell my parents about my **REAL SUMMER PLANS.**

I've got this in the bag!

SATURDAY

My life is ruined!

My parents came home last night talking about how the teacher showed them the **GREAT ESSAY** I wrote.

'I never knew you liked camp so much, son,' Dad said.

'Yes, honey. Why didn't you tell us you loved camp so much? We were going to give you the summer to do whatever you wanted,' my mum said. 'Now that we know you love camp so much, we **SIGNED YOU UP** to go to camp this summer. There was a camp representative at the parent-teacher conference last night, so we signed you up right away.'

'We even went and placed a non-refundable deposit for it too, son,' Dad said. 'So, congratulations, you're going to camp!'

OMG!

My life is totally ruined! Now I'm going to spend my scare-cation in the Swamp Biome at camp. Oh man, this is terrible!

What am I going to do?!

I decided to ask Steve some advice on how to get out of my **TERRIBLE SITUATION.** I found Steve in a cave crafting some fireworks.

Man, these things are loud!

All of a sudden, 'BOOOOMMM!'

All that was left of him were his tools and his weapons.

A few minutes later, Steve walked into the cave **BEHIND ME.** I totally understand how he does that trick now.

'Hey, Steve!'

'Wassup, Zombie?' Steve said.

'I have a question for you.'

'Shoot!' Steve said.

So, I picked up his Bow and Arrow

and I shot him.

'Ow! What'd you do that for?' shouted Steve.

'You told me to shoot,' I said.

'Forget about it. **SO...** what's your question?'

'My mum and dad are making me go to camp this summer,' I said. 'But I don't want to go. I've got to find a way out of it and I need your help.'

'Why are they sending you to camp?' Steve asked.

'Well, I kind of told them I wanted to go.'

'And now, you don't want to go?' Steve asked.

'No, I never wanted to go,' I said.

Steve just looked at me... confused.

'Well, I thought if I wrote an essay about how much I wanted to go to camp, my mum and dad wouldn't send me to camp,' I said.

After I said it out loud, I realised **HOW DUMB** that idea was.

'It sure made sense at the time,' I said.

'So, you want to get out of camp but your parents think you really want to go?' Steve asked.

'Yeah.'

'Well, you could always get in trouble and they'll **PUNISH YOU** by taking away your summer camp,' Steve said.

Man, Steve is so smart. That was the best idea I have ever heard.

So, I've got to get in trouble so

that my parents will punish me by taking camp away. I can do that. I just have to decide on a class that I can fail in this term and they'll punish me for sure if that happens.

See... this is why I **ALWAYS** go to Steve when I need some good advice!

☀ SUNDAY ☀

So I figured out how I was going to fail one of my classes.

The Annual School Science Fair is supposed to be this week. Everybody in my science class is supposed to bring **A PROJECT.** And my mum and dad have been reminding me about it throughout the school term.

So I was thinking... if I make the worst science project ever, then

I'll flunk my science class for sure! Then my parents will ground me and not let me go to camp.

So, I need to come up with the **WORST SCIENCE EXPERIMENT** ever.

Let me see...

I could enter my booger collection.

Nah... I did that last year and I still passed my class.

Or I could enter one of my smelly gym socks. There's a lot of science going on there.

Nah. Knowing my science teacher, he'll probably give me an 'A' for creativity or something.

Or I could dissect my little brother and show that little brothers really are rotten to the core.

Nah. Even though it would be a lot of fun, I would probably have a hard time holding him down.

No. It needed to be the worst SCIENCE EXPERIMENT ever known to Zombie-kind.

I know! I'll enter Steve, a Human,

as my science experiment,
I thought.

Oh man, that would get me a failing grade for sure.

Either that or it would scare the nightlights out of my science teacher and all of the other kids. Then I would really get in a lot of trouble.

Wow, **SUMMER SCARE-CATION** here I come!

M☀NDAY

I told Steve about my plans for the Science Fair and he was all in.

'So, I'm going to stick some electrodes to your forehead and neck. Then, I'm going to throw a switch, and you're going to come to life,' I said.

'You mean like in Frankenstein?' Steve asked.

'FRANKEN-WHO?'

'Frankenstein. You know, the

story about the mad scientist that collected body parts and sewed them together. Then he shocked the body full of lightning and it came to life,' Steve said.

'Never heard of him,' I said. 'But, anyway, the **SCIENCE FAIR** is on Wednesday. You just have to meet me before school, outside of the gym, and I'll let you in through the back. Got it?'

'Got it,' Steve said.

This idea was sure to give me a failing grade.

Then I would be free from my trip to 'PRISON CAMP', and I would be able to enjoy my summer.

This was a really great idea, I thought.

Wow, I never knew I was so smart.

Yeah me.

TUESDAY

Today, Creepy was telling me all about how excited he was to be going to camp. He told me that they were going to have a big **TALENT SHOW** this year and he was going to be part of a band.

'I didn't know you could play an instrument,' I said to Creepy.

'Yeah, I play a mean set of drums,' Creepy said.

Now, I was going to ask him how

he plays drums without arms, but then I thought some things were best left alone.

I told the guys my idea for the Science Fair.

'Whoa, that's really cool,' they said.

The guys weren't the smartest bunch, so if they liked it, I was sure that the teacher was going to hate my idea and fail my project.

Later at home, I prepared my **MACHINE** with electrodes and everything. I took the extra

car battery from the garage
and connected it. It started
SPARKING and making noise.

'MUAHAHAHAHA!!!' I said real loud.

I thought I might as well act the
part and make it look real.

So, I was all set.

When I came down to dinner, my
mum and dad asked me about the
Science Fair.

'What are you going to do for
your project this year?' Dad asked.
'I hope you're not entering your

BOOGER COLLECTION

again. I'm sorry buddy, but a booger collection is not exactly Science Fair material. Especially since everyone has one.'

'Don't worry, Dad. This year I went all out,' I said. 'My project is going to be a real winner.'

'Honey, I'm so proud of you,' Mum said. 'And, if you win, we were thinking of giving you an extra week of camp as a reward.'

'Yeah!' I said, knowing full well I was going to flunk miserably.

I would be spending my summer playing **VIDEO GAMES** and eating tons of cake.

WEDNESDAY

They said that a famous Zombie
was visiting the school and was
going to help judge the Science Fair
this year.

*That's great, I thought, now I
know I'll definitely fail.*

So I got everything ready and I
let Steve in through the back of
the gym. I had Steve lie down on
a table and I put a **BLANKET**
over him. Then I rolled him out
next to my electrode machine.

The famous visiting Zombie was really tall. Almost as tall as my friend Mutant. He went around with the science teacher, judging all of the other Science Fair projects.

Look how tall Mutant is!

He didn't look too impressed with any of them though.

Great, then he'll really hate mine, I thought.

My experiment was the last one to get judged. So when the famous Zombie and the science teacher came to my table, I got into character.

'**MUAHAHAHAHAHA!!!**' I said, 'Now I will bring this human back to life. MUAHAHAHAHAHA!!!'

I threw the switch and all of the lights went out in the gym. My

ELECTRODE MACHINE was shooting sparks and lighting up the whole place.

'RISE, MY CREATURE! RISE!'

Right on cue, Steve sat up from the table.

'IT'S ALIVE! IT'S ALLLIIIIIIIVE!' I said in my crazy scientist voice.

Steve stood up and he stretched his arms out like a Zombie and said, 'UUURRGGHH!!!'

All of a sudden, the mob kids started running and screaming out of the gym.

'IT'S A **HUMAN!**' they screamed, as Steve chased after them.

Man, it's working, I thought. This is a disaster! I'm going to flunk this class for sure.

'MUAHAHAHAHAHA!!!'

All of a sudden, the lights came back on. The visiting famous Zombie was standing right in front of me.

As he stared at me, he did the weirdest thing ever. He raised his hand and wiped a tear from his eye.

'That was the most amazing thing I have ever seen!' he said. Then he ran out of the gym sobbing.

My science teacher came over to me and said, 'Congratulations, Zombie. That was the most **AUTHENTIC RE-ENACTMENT** of Frankenstein's experiment that I have ever seen. But how did you know that Frankenstein's Creation was going to visit today? I only heard about it this morning...'

I just looked at him... confused.

The more I thought about it,
Steve did look a lot like the
famous Zombie! They both had the
electrodes stuck on their head.

Then I dreaded what he was going
to say next.

'Everyone, everyone! The winner
of this year's Science Fair, for
outstanding creativity, authenticity
and imagination, goes to Zack
Zombie, for his project—The Rise of
Frankenstein's Creation!'

Everybody in the gym started
**APPLAUDING AND
CHEERING.**

'How do you feel, son?' my science
teacher asked me.

'Great,' I said. But all I could
think about was my parents
adding another week to my
summer 'prison camp' sentence.

THURSDAY

My parents took me to The **WOKING DEAD** Chinese Restaurant to celebrate me winning the Science Fair.

'We're so proud of you, son,' Dad said. 'You're a chip off the old block.'

'Maybe he can work with you at the Nuclear Waste Plant for the summer,' Mum said. 'That way he'll be able to develop his scientific talent.'

I just tried to bury my sorrow in my Zombie egg roll.

'So, son,' Dad said. 'I just put another non-refundable deposit in for another week at camp for you. I don't know how we're going to afford it. But you're worth it.'

'Maybe we should send him to science camp too, this summer!' Mum said.

I **THREW UP** my egg roll.

'Wow, look how excited he is,' Mum said.

FRIDAY

One good thing came out of winning the Science Fair, Mum and Dad said I could go to a sleepover at Skelee's house to celebrate.

So Slimey, Creepy and I went over to Skelee's house for a **SLEEPOVER** movie night. All of the guys congratulated me on my Science Fair win.

Then Creepy started talking more about how lucky I was that I get to go to camp for an extra week.

'There's going to be a competition against the camp next to us,' Creepy said. 'We've lost every year since I've been there. But with your science skills, I think we can really beat them this year.'

'Guys, I don't want to talk about it anymore,' I said. 'What movie are we watching tonight, anyway?'

'**CREEPAWAY CAMP 3:**
Terror in the Woods,' Skelee said. 'I heard it was really good.'

Oh brother...

SATURDAY

I went back to Steve to ask for more advice about how to get out of camp.

'Congratulations on your win,' Steve said **SARCASTICALLY.**

I just looked at him, depressed.

'Now what am I going to do?' I said. 'My mum and dad are going to give me two weeks at camp and I don't know what to do.'

'Don't worry. You still have plenty

of time to mess things up,' Steve said. 'Don't you have any **BIG EXAMS** coming up soon?'

'Yeah! I have a big Scare Class exam on Monday. Hey, if I mess that up, then my parents will ground me for sure!' I said. 'The only problem is that the exam is going to be graded on how well we can scare Villagers. And Villagers are really easy to scare. They're scared of everything.'

'Well, if you make them laugh, then there's no way they can be scared,' Steve said.

Wow. Steve is a genius. Where does he come up with this stuff?

'That's a great idea. But I'm going to have to come up with something to make them laugh,' I said.

'I've got a **GREAT ROUTINE** you can use,' Steve said. 'Every time I do it, it always makes my friends laugh.'

'Thanks, Steve. I really appreciate your help.'

So Steve showed me his routine and we practised it for a few hours.

Man, I can't wait to do this

routine on my Scare test on Monday. I'm going to have those Villagers in **STITCHES.**

Summer scare-cation, here I come!

✳ SUNDAY ✳

Today I spent the whole day practising the comedy routine at home in front of a mirror.

I never thought of myself as a **COMEDIAN.** I tried to tell a joke once. It went like this...

Why was the Zombie afraid to cross the road?

Because he lost his guts!

I loved that joke! I wasn't sure why, but every time I told it, nobody laughed.

But I knew since Steve came up with this routine, it must be really funny.

The good thing was that there was not a lot of talking in this routine, just **SILLY MOVEMENTS.** And I could tell while practising in the mirror, that it would be really funny.

I couldn't wait to try it out on the Villagers tomorrow.

M✳NDAY

I woke up late today, so I had to rush out of bed and head out straight to school. I didn't even get a chance to eat breakfast.

I didn't care because I was just so excited to mess up my **SCARE EXAM** and get my life back this summer.

I made it to Ms Bones' Scare Class when she said, 'Kids, remember, this exam will count towards

50% of your grade. So make sure you **GIVE IT** your all when you go out and scare those Villagers today.'

Not me, I thought, I'm going to get those Villagers laughing so hard, they won't be scared at all.

When we got to the village, all the other kids picked a Villager to scare. And the other kids did really well.

But then it was my turn. I picked a Villager that I saw picking crops.

Steve also gave me some music to

go with the routine, so I turned on the speakers and jumped out of the bushes.

'Everybody Dance Now!'

I started doing my routine and it was good! The Villager **WASN'T SCARED** at all!

I was really getting into my routine and soon, more and more Villagers gathered around me. I was really getting the hang of this!

Soon, the entire village was gathered around me and they were into it too.

My 'groovy' dance moves ←⟡⟡⟡⟡

'Hey guys, check out what Zombie is doing!' one of the mob kids yelled.

Then all of the mob kids jumped out of the bushes at once. All of a sudden, the entire village went crazy and the Villagers started running and screaming.

'It's the Zombie Apocalypse!' a Villager yelled.

'AAAAHHHH!!!' was all I heard as all of the Villagers SCATTERED to their homes.

Ms Bones was shocked.

'You scared the entire village all at once!' she said. 'That was the most amazing thing I have ever seen!'

Then she said, 'You get an A+ for your Scare test and for the entire class. Congratulations, Zombie!'

Man, I really hate my life.

TUESDAY

Today my parents took me to the Drool and Gruel diner to celebrate my **A+** on my Scare exam.

'Son, you never stop surprising us,' Dad said. 'We talked to your teacher and she said that your Scare technique was so good that it reminded her of a re-enactment of the Zombie Apocalypse! It was the best thing she had ever seen. You scared every Villager in that town.'

'Thanks Dad,' I said as I buried my sorrow in a Drool Shake.

'Honey, you should tell him about the surprise,' Mum said.

'WHAT SURPRISE?' I asked.

'Well, son. Ms Bones was so impressed with your work that she spoke to the Principal. And the Principal agreed to sponsor you for an extra week of camp as a reward. Isn't that amazing?!' Dad said.

I threw up my Drool Shake.

'Look how excited he is, honey. He

can't even keep his **DROOL**
SHAKE down,' Mum said.

Life is so unfair.

WEDNESDAY

Well, even though it's been a crazy few days, the one cool thing is that the yearbook will come out today.

Man, I can't wait! I've been looking forward to seeing my yearbook picture since we took our photos on Picture Day. I bet I'm going to look **REAL GOOD.**

If I'm lucky, I'll even look like an eighth grader!

I'm going to get everybody to sign

my yearbook too.

They're probably going to write something like 'The COOLEST ZOMBIE in school', or 'The Zombie most likely to succeed'.

Or something cool like that.

Mum said that yearbook pictures are great because it's a way that people can remember you for the rest of your life. When she pulls out her yearbook I can tell it brings back really great memories for her... even though it was a really, really, REALLY long time ago.

Dad told me not to get my hopes up too high, though. I think it's because my dad's yearbook picture looks like he was one of the smartest kids in school.

'Your yearbook pictures are only **A SNAPSHOT** of a very short period of your life,' he said. 'You always outgrow those pictures anyway.'

I don't know how much I believe that last thing he said. Since under his yearbook picture it said, 'The most likely to work in a Nuclear Waste Plant'.

They weren't wrong there!

I think I'm going to get extra pictures printed out to give out to people. I'm going to get some for grandma. I'm going to get a few for Sally. And I'll probably need a few for my photo spread in **ZQ MAGAZINE**...

THURSDAY

OMG!

My life is officially over.

As soon as I opened my yearbook I saw my picture...

The 'blech' had taken all the green out of my face... my skin was white. **I LOOKED HUMAN!**

I couldn't believe it.

I looked terrible!

My picture was so awful that all the kids in school were laughing at me when I walked down the hallway.

When I wasn't paying attention, somebody wrote in my yearbook, 'The Zombie most likely to be mistaken for a Human'.

Somebody else wrote, 'The Zombie most likely to work at the Chum Bucket'.

Somebody even wrote, 'The Zombie most likely to host a **REALITY TV SHOW**'.

When I got to class, Ms Bones

had all of the yearbook pictures scanned on her computer. So she had a giant picture of somebody in the class projected on the screen every few seconds, with a speech bubble asking the class a question.

When my picture came up, the question next to it said, 'How scary am I?'

All of the mob kids burst out laughing.

It was the most EMBARRASSING day ever.

FRIDAY

I went to see Steve today. Even though being a Scare School Zombie kid is really tough, it's really great to have a friend like Steve I can talk to.

'What's the matter, Zombie?' Steve asked. 'You look really blue.'

'Really? I'm usually a **NICE SHADE** of green.'

'No, I mean you look really sad,' Steve said.

'Well, this is going to be the worst summer ever!' I said. 'Not only are my parents going to send me to camp for **THREE WEEKS** but I got my yearbook picture back and it's the worst ever!'

'Really? Let me see,' he said.

I gave him my yearbook and he took a look at it.

Then he burst out laughing.

'It's not funny, you know,' I said.

'Sorry. I didn't mean to laugh. It's just that you look like a really famous person from where I'm from,' Steve said.

'Really? He looks like that and he's famous?'

'Yeah, he's **REALLY POPULAR** too,' he said. 'But you're lucky. At least it's not as bad as my picture.'

Steve showed me his yearbook picture.

Steve's yearbook picture

'Whoa.'

'Yeah, I like to make funny faces for my yearbook pictures,' he said. 'I just figured that if I can laugh at myself, then I really don't care if other people laugh at me either.'

'But don't you care that this is the way people are going to REMEMBER YOU for the rest of your life?' I said.

'My real friends are going to remember me for more than my dumb yearbook picture,' he said.

'Yeah, I guess you're right! You know, now that I look at it, my yearbook picture is kind of funny,' I said.

And then we both started laughing.

Man, every time I talk to Steve, I always feel better.

I don't know how I would've been able to get through my Zombie **SCHOOL LIFE** without a friend like him. I just wish that Steve could help me find a way out of going to camp.

SATURDAY

I had a daymare today that my parents abandoned me at camp.

I walked into a room where some mob kids were quietly making some lanyards and MACARONI PICTURES. All of a sudden, the kids grabbed me and wrapped the lanyards around my neck. Then another group of kids glued macaroni and googly eyes on my head in the shape of a smiley face.

I ran out of there and ran to the

camp food hall to hide. Then, while I was there, the camp food suddenly came to life and attacked me.

I ran as fast as I could into a group of camp counsellors.

'Help me, please,' I said.

'Sure, we'll help you. We love helping ourselves to the kids at camp...'

Suddenly, all of the camp counsellors turned Human and they started saying, 'Braaaaiiiinnnss!'

They wanted to **EAT MY BRAIN!**

So, I ran to the nurse's office to get help. The camp nurse pulled out a huge tongue depressor and said, 'Open your mouth and say "Ahhhh!"'

Right before my eyes she turned into a rotten, flesh-eating Witch that wanted to have me for lunch.

'Watch me open my mouth and say "AHAHAHAHA!"' she cackled, as her mouth opened up really big and she swallowed me whole!

THEN I WOKE UP.

Oh man. I've got to find a way out of this camp situation, I thought.

If I didn't, I was going to be eaten by the camp counsellors, the nurse or the camp food.

There must be some way that I could fail in a class and get my parents to punish me by taking camp away. But the only thing I had left for the school year was my **DUMB PRESENTATION** for mob history class.

The only problem was that it didn't count that much towards my grade. So even if I skip it, I would still pass the class.

But you know, we were supposed

to do our presentations in front of the whole school assembly. And everybody, including the Principal and all of the parents, was going to be there.

If I made it the dumbest, craziest and the most diabolical presentation ever, they're going to have to flunk me. But it had to be really bad. So bad that I might be forced to change schools after I did it.

Now I just had to come up with an idea for my presentation.

I bet Steve would have a **GREAT IDEA!**

☀ SUNDAY ☀

I met up with Steve and I told him about the mob history class presentation.

'You know, you can do a presentation about where Zombies come from,' Steve said.

'Where do they come from?' I asked. 'I've been trying to get my mum to tell me but every time I bring it up, she KEEPS CHANGING the subject.'

'I've heard stories,' Steve said.

'Most of the stuff I know comes from movies.'

'Well, if there is one thing I know about movies, it's that they're **REALLY ACCURATE,**' I said.

So Steve and I spent the whole night putting my presentation together. I even got the other guys to agree to help act out different parts in it.

Man, we added so much crazy stuff into the presentation that it would probably get me banned from school.

Hey, a kid's gotta do what he's gotta do... especially when the **SUMMER SCARE-CATION** was on the line.

M✱NDAY

Well, today we're having our end of year assembly.

We're going to be showing our presentations to the whole seventh grade class, including all of the teachers, the Principal and the parents. My presentation is ready. And the guys are ready.

I think this presentation is going to go down in history as the most **INFAMOUS PRESENTATION** ever given at a mob school. It could actually get me arrested.

But hey, as long as I don't have to go to camp, that's **ALL THAT MATTERS.**

Here goes nothing...

MONDAY SPECIAL NIGHT ENTRY

I think it worked!

When it was my turn to do my presentation, I could tell that people were looking forward to something like what all the other kids did. The other kids spoke on very basic topics. So I knew my presentation would have a good amount of **SHOCK VALUE.**

Before I started my presentation, they turned off all the lights, except for a spotlight on the stage. I walked out onto the stage and I started **TELLING THE TALE** of the 'Untold Story of the Origin of Zombies'.

It went like this:

Where do Zombies come from? No one really knows. But after some extensive investigative Zombie journalism, I've discovered the truth.

It all began when the Human government decided that they wanted to create stronger soldiers. They had lost too many battles and now they wanted to win every war that they fought. So they approached some soldiers in their army to join a **SPECIAL SECRET PROJECT.** The only requirement was that the soldiers that were chosen had no living relatives. This way, no one could identify and claim their bodies if something went wrong.

So, they exposed these soldiers to an experimental virus that would enhance their abilities and make them into super soldiers. The experiment seemed to be working, for a while. Then, something terrible happened...

The soldiers went crazy and

they were horribly disfigured.
Ultimately, the experiment claimed
their lives. But when the soldiers
were being prepared for burial,
they suddenly came back to life.

They were not only walking but
they had enhanced strength,
enhanced sense of smell and
enhanced hearing. They attacked
the soldiers in charge of burying
them. And the recently bitten
soldiers also transformed into the
LIVING DEAD.

Before long, the entire army
base was contaminated with the
virus. Once everyone on the base

was exposed, the virus mutated and the soldiers began having an overwhelming craving for something warm and mushy.

They longed for **BRAINS!**

Soon, the army of the living dead found their way to an unsuspecting town nearby in search of brains. They attacked that town, biting anything that moved, both Human and animal. Soon that town was overrun. The virus spread from town to town and city to city, until the entire world was contaminated.

It was the first Zombie Apocalypse.

After hundreds of years had passed, the Zombies started to **EVOLVE** and began developing intelligent thoughts.

They began forming villages... and then towns... and then entire cities of Zombies were created. The Zombies made great advances in health and science and became highly advanced technologically.

But, eventually the Zombies' appetite for brains and warm flesh gave way to an even greater craving...

the craving for CAKE!

Their overwhelming desire for cake resulted in an explosive rise in the **BAKING INDUSTRY.** Cake shops began springing up on every corner of every Zombie city street. They just couldn't get enough!

The Human race began growing again, too.

Human villages of farmers and miners began springing up. And because the Zombies were now a peaceful mob, they coexisted with the Humans, by staying away from them.

But soon, the Zombies' resources began to **BECOME SCARCE,** especially the cake.

So Zombies began scaring Villagers in order to get the supplies they needed, especially the highly valued resource of cake.

Now Zombies send their kids to Scare School to train their children from a very young age. They train them on how to effectively scare Humans in order to get their needed supplies, especially cake.

And so it has been until today.

Thank you.

The entire audience was **DEAD QUIET.** Everyone just sat there with a stunned look on their face. They started walking out of the auditorium in silence, with their heads hanging low. Mum and Dad were really quiet on the way home, too.

I finally did it.

I was definitely going to fail my mob history class presentation for sure. Who knows, I might even get kicked out of Scare School. But, all I knew was that I could say **GOODBYE TO CAMP.**

It was going to be the best summer ever!

TUESDAY

I must be cursed.

No matter what I try, I just can't get out of going to camp!

I know someone, somewhere, must have had a talk with a Witch who **PUT A CURSE** on me. I bet it was big-mouth Jeff. Or maybe it was Mike Magma. He probably has a Witch for a ghoulfriend and she has cast a big hex on me.

Whatever it was, nothing I tried

seemed to work.

I thought for sure that my presentation would get everyone at school so mad that they would definitely kick me out of school. How could I know there would be reporters at the school yesterday? And how could I know that someone would record it and put it on the **ZOMBIE-NET?**

But there I am, on the front page of today's paper.

'Possible Zombie Missing Link Discovered by Genius Zombie Kid.'

And the recording went viral. Now everyone in **THE OVERWORLD** is talking about it. The Principal even talked about making me the seventh grade valedictorian.

And my parents were so proud that they promised they would pay for me to go to camp every year for the **REST OF MY SCHOOL LIFE.**

I don't get it.

I mean, I just don't get it.

WEDNESDAY

Today all of the guys were talking about their summer plans again.

Creepy started telling me about how excited he was that I get to go to camp for a whole three weeks.

'They're going to have a lot of team building games and cool sports stuff,' he said. 'We can even **BUNK TOGETHER.** I hope you don't mind, but I hiss sometimes when I sleep.'

I don't know how I feel about the last thing Creepy said.

I started feeling a **LITTLE SAD** because I was going to miss most of my friends this summer. Sally had already left last week on her summer scare-cation. Her parents planned to take her on a world tour of all the Biomes.

Man, it sure must be cool having rich parents, I thought.

I told Sally how depressed I was about going to camp before she left.

'Don't worry about it, Zombie. You might just have a great time. When I went to camp, I thought I would hate it too. But I ended up making some of the best friends I've ever had,' she said.

'What about the **KILLER COUNSELLORS** and the rotten flesh-eating nurses?' I asked.

'That's just your imagination talking,' she said. 'Besides, the only thing that could kill you at camp is the camp food. Just make sure you pack lots of snacks.'

I wasn't sure if she was joking when she said that last part or if she was serious.

I guess it would be fun **WRITING LETTERS** to my friends over the summer. And I could always call them.

My mum said that if I filled my summer with lots of activities, scare-cation would go by quickly and I would see my friends in no time.

So, I'd better get used to making a whole lot of lanyards and macaroni pictures.

❊ THURSDAY ❊

We got our report cards from Scare School today. I never thought I would be sad about getting **STRAIGHT A'S** in all my classes, though.

Which was really weird because I had never gotten an A in any class. C's and D's were more my style. I did get a B once. But I think it was because the gym teacher felt sorry for me.

I'm the Zombie that teachers always write on my report card, 'He's got so much potential'. I figured that as long as the teachers know, why waste time trying to prove it?

Anyway, it feels really weird not having to hide my REPORT CARD from my parents for a change.

No trying to erase my grade, or intercepting the teacher's Z-mail or answering the phone using my mum's voice. I can actually just come home and hand my report card to my mum and dad.

Still feels really weird, though.

Today we had the seventh grade mob award ceremony, too. That's when all the seventh grade mob kids get an award for not flunking out of Scare School, and making it to eighth grade.

For some reason, they made us wear these really funny caps and gowns.

Slimey had a hard time finding a cap and gown his size. So he used a **PIANO COVER** instead.

Creepy had a hard time putting his on. I think it's because he doesn't have any arms.

You know, that's probably why he walks around naked all the time.

Skelee looked really good in his cap and gown. He said he didn't even have to buy one. His uncle had his old one lying around in the closet.

Though we still don't know what the **SICKLE** is for.

But we all got cool awards.

Slimey got the 'Most Well-Rounded Student' award.

Creepy got the 'Most Sensitive Student' award. I think that

meant that he was sent home the most this school year.

Skelee got the 'Most Transparent Student' award.

And I got the 'Most Shocking Turnaround of Any Student, Ever' award.

Didn't really understand what that meant but it was cool.

FRIDAY

Today was our last day of Scare School.

They decided to have a CARNIVAL for us, which I thought was really cool. There was some really awesome rides, mob game booths, rotten candy, zombie clowns (which are really creepy by the way), a Scary-Go-Round and a Ferris Wheel.

Skelee and I really liked the Scary-Go-Round.

Slimey liked the rotten candy.

Creepy said he liked the **FERRIS WHEEL.** He said he just loves the thrill of being up so high.

Sometimes I really don't understand what Creepy says... everybody knows he's afraid of heights.

But, even though I have to go to camp in a few weeks, I'm looking forward to having fun on these last few days of **FREEDOM** with my friends.

FRIDAY NIGHT SPECIAL ENTRY

The carnival was a lot of fun. But the CRAZIEST thing happened towards the end of the night.

Skelee and I decided to go on the Scary-Go-Round one last time. I told Slimey to stick with Creepy so that Creepy wouldn't have to go on the Ferris Wheel by himself.

But something happened.

Slimey was probably quite

distracted by the rotten candy machine because somehow he lost Creepy. Before we knew it, there was a lot of screaming and yelling coming from the Ferris Wheel.

We ran over there, and saw a **BIG CROWD.** Somehow the Ferris Wheel got stuck and there were mob kids stuck in the seats.

I didn't want to look up... but I did.

And there was Creepy all the way at the top, all by himself. I could tell he was scared, which meant trouble for everybody.

I went to the Enderman that was operating the ride.

'Hey, somebody needs to climb up there to get him down!' I said.

'Nah man, I **JUST WORK HERE,** bro,' he said.

Uuuurrrgghhh! Teenagers! I thought.

I started to come up with a plan. I would go up and rescue Creepy myself! But I realised that if I climbed up there, I wouldn't be able to climb down with Creepy.

I decided to climb up there anyway

and see if I could calm Creepy down. So I climbed all the way to the top, which was really scary.

'Hey, Creepy,' I said. 'How are you doing, buddy?'

'I'm **REALLY SCARED,** Zombie. I want my mum.'

Wow. This was next level scared for Creepy!

'Don't worry, buddy, I'm here. I won't leave you alone,' I said.

I tried to distract him from being up so high, so I talked about camp.

'I can't wait to go to camp with you, Creepy,' I said. 'We're going to have so much fun. We're going to make lanyards and macaroni pictures. We're going to do a lot of **TEAM BUILDING** exercises. And we can bunk together in the same cabin. Camp is going to be a lot of fun, isn't it?'

'To be honest, Zombie, I really don't like camp,' Creepy said.

'Really?'

'Yeah. I feel so lonely there. And all the kids just pick on me all the time. I think it's because I'm really bad at all of the sports and stuff. And I'm going to miss my mum and dad so much. And I'm really going to miss you guys a lot, too.'

'Wow, Creepy. I didn't know,' I said.

'But now that I know you're going, Zombie, it's going to be so much more fun,' Creepy said and he **STARTED SMILING** and stopped hissing.

Then, all of a sudden the Ferris Wheel started moving again.

We got off the Ferris Wheel and a

Mobulance was waiting there for me and Creepy. The **MOBULANCE** nurse put a blanket around Creepy and I and gave us some cake. She was really nice.

'Thank you,' we said.

'You're welcome. That was really brave of you to go up there and help your friend. I wish there were more kids like you around,' she said.

'Hey, I know you!' Creepy said. 'You're the nurse that works at our camp every summer.'

'Yeah, I am! Creepy, right?' she said.

Creepy started turning red and green. I think he had a crush on her or something.

'Wow, you're the nurse at camp?' I asked.

'Yep. I've worked at camp every year for the past few years,' she said.

I wanted to ask her if she had a craving for **ROTTEN FLESH,** but she walked away to take care of the other mob kids.

'She remembered my name!' Creepy said excitedly.

I went to go visit Steve today to tell him all about what happened at the carnival.

'Wow, Zombie,' he said, 'That was really cool. You really went out on **A LIMB** for Creepy.'

'But I have all my limbs.'

'No, I mean that you really came through for Creepy when he needed a friend,' Steve said.

'Yeah. And you know, even though

I don't want to go to camp, I think I'm going to go just so that Creepy can have a friend around. He said that he gets **REALLY LONELY** at camp.'

'Who's going to be there for you?' Steve said.

'I guess it doesn't matter... it's only for a few weeks anyway,' I said.

'Well, it matters to me,' Steve said. 'That's why I'm going with you.'

'Are you serious?'

'Hey, that's what friends are for,' Steve said. 'Besides, we can always sneak out and bother some Witches or something.'

Wow. Steve is like one of the **BEST FRIENDS** I could ever have. Which is weird... because he's Human.

But I guess it doesn't matter if you're a Human, Slime, Skeleton or Creeper. All that matters is a true friend will always be there when you need them.

So, I'm going to camp in a few weeks. But I'm not going alone. I will be going with two of the best friends any Zombie could ask for.

Plus, we're going to need all the help we can get if we're going to survive against the **BRAIN-EATING, KILLER COUNSELLORS...**

And the camp food monster.

DIARY OF A MINECRAFT ZOMBIE

Take a peek into the diary of Zack Zombie. He's just like any other kid, except he's a lot more **DEAD**!

COLLECT THEM ALL!

 ☑ GOT IT!
 ☑ GOT IT!
 ☑ GOT IT!
 ☑ GOT IT!
 ☑ GOT IT!

 ☑ GOT IT!
 ☑ GOT IT!
 ☑ GOT IT!
 ☑ GOT IT!
 ☑ GOT IT!

DIARY OF A MINECRAFT ZOMBIE BOOK 11 — INSIDES OUT	DIARY OF A MINECRAFT ZOMBIE BOOK 12 — PIXELMON GONE!	DIARY OF A MINECRAFT ZOMBIE BOOK 13 — FRIDAY NIGHT FRIGHTS	DIARY OF A MINECRAFT ZOMBIE BOOK — CLOUDY WITH A CHANCE OF APOCALYPSE	DIARY OF A MINECRAFT ZOMBIE BOOK — ATTACK OF THE GNOMES
☑ GOT IT!	☑ GOT IT!	☑ GOT IT!	☑ GOT IT!	☑ GOT IT!

DIARY OF A MINECRAFT ZOMBIE BOOK 16 — DOWN THE DRAIN	DIARY OF A MINECRAFT ZOMBIE — ZOMBIE'S EXCELLENT ADVENTURE	DIARY OF A MINECRAFT ZOMBIE — IN TOO DEEP	DIARY OF A MINECRAFT ZOMBIE — ZOMBIES VS ALIENS	DIARY OF A MINECRAFT ZOMBIE BOOK 20 — MOB MASH
☑ GOT IT!	☑ GOT IT!	☑ GOT IT!	☑ GOT IT!	☑ GOT IT!

DIARY OF A MINECRAFT ZOMBIE BOOK 21 — CARNIVAL CHAOS	DIARY OF A MINECRAFT ZOMBIE BOOK 22 — THROUGH THE WORMHOLE	DIARY OF A MINECRAFT ZOMBIE BOOK 23 — ROYAL RECALL	DIARY OF A MINECRAFT ZOMBIE BOOK 24 — SUPER STAKEOUT	DIARY OF A MINECRAFT ZOMBIE BOOK 25 — MISSION POSSIBLE
☑ GOT IT!	☑ GOT IT!	☑ GOT IT!	☑ GOT IT!	☑ GOT IT!

DIARY OF A MINECRAFT ZOMBIE BOOK 26 — CURSE OF THE STOLEN DIAMOND	DIARY OF A MINECRAFT ZOMBIE BOOK 27 — PIRATES OF THE LOST OCEAN TEMPLE	DIARY OF A MINECRAFT ZOMBIE BOOK 28 — THE ABOMINABLE SNOW GOLEM	DIARY OF A MINECRAFT ZOMBIE — PET SHOW PANDEMONIUM	DIARY OF A MINECRAFT ZOMBIE BOOK 30 — MOB FU MASTER
☑ GOT IT!	☑ GOT IT!	☑ GOT IT!	☐ GOT IT!	☐ GOT IT!

COLLECT THEM ALL!

DIARY OF A MINECRAFT ENDERMAN

☐ **GOT IT!**

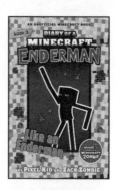

☐ **GOT IT!**

☐ **GOT IT!**

☐ **GOT IT!**